The Bradford family ADVENTURES

Daniel and the Big Blizzard

by
Jeremy Grice and
Jerry B. Jenkins

MOODY PRESS
CHICAGO

To Hannah Van Orman

Contents

1

Big Plans

Daniel and Yolanda Bradford were so excited they could hardly stand it. They were going to a weekend camp-out during spring vacation with the kids from their church.

Daniel, a sixth-grader, and Yolanda, in fourth, knew a lot about Camp Hickory. They had each been there the summer before. Yolanda had gone to girls' camp and Daniel to the camp for boys, but they had never been there together.

Better yet, for the Thursday through Sunday camp-out, they wouldn't be staying in the cabins. They would be outdoors, in tents, a dozen of them. There would be campfires, games in the dark, singing, and all kinds of fun. Don and Violet Forester would be in charge. They were everybody's favorites.

The Foresters didn't have children. But they made up for that by treating all the junior-age Sunday-school kids as if they were their own. Don was a tall, skinny, ruddy-faced man who was a star on the church softball team. He had sparkling eyes and a shock of dark hair he could never keep combed.

He was full of fun and mischief, and his deep, bass

voice was always teasing someone or laughing at someone's joke, whether it was really funny or not. Don was a great storyteller, from scary stories just for fun to serious Bible stories that had a message.

His wife had long, light brown hair and was very quiet. Daniel wished she'd talk more. When she did, it seemed she had good things to say. She was very warm and loving with the kids, but she spent more time teaching the girls than the boys. Yolanda loved her, maybe because Mrs. Forester had been adopted, too.

Ever since a few weeks after Yolanda joined the Bradford family, Violet Forester had been one of her favorite people. Yolanda wasn't sure at first how she would like going to church. But it wasn't long before she was the first one ready every Sunday morning.

There were about forty kids in the church in the fourth, fifth, and sixth grades; so three high school kids were going to help with the campers. One was Jim Bradford, Daniel and Yolanda's brother, a basketball star.

Their sister, Maryann, would be gone all weekend with her parents to a cheerleaders' competition. Just before they left early that Thursday afternoon, Mrs. Bradford finished helping Daniel and Yolanda pack.

"You're looking forward to this, aren't you, Yo-Yo?"

Yolanda nodded, but her smile was weak.

"Are you a little afraid?"

She nodded. "A little."

"You know Mr. and Mrs. Forester will watch out for you. And Daniel and Jim will be there. And I'm packing lots of warm clothes in case the weather turns cold."

"*I'm* even a little scared," Daniel admitted. "But mostly I'm just excited."

"I want to stay in Violet's tent," Yolanda said.

"Please call her Mrs. Forester," Mrs. Bradford said.

"She wants us to call her Violet," Yolanda said. "Honest!"

Daniel nodded.

Mrs. Bradford shrugged. "If the weather gets too bad, I

hope they'll either bring you home or get you inside somewhere."

"They will, dear," Mr. Bradford said. "Don't worry."

But both Daniel and Yolanda knew she would. She always did. She never thought anyone could take care of her children the way she could.

Mr. and Mrs. Bradford and the pretty, dark-haired Maryann would be traveling several hundred miles to get to the cheerleading clinic. So they pulled out a little before two in the afternoon.

Jim and the two younger children would be leaving for the church parking lot a few minutes before six o'clock. From there it would be a three-hour bus ride to the camp. There the first activity would be pitching tents, then singing and talking around a roaring campfire.

Daniel couldn't keep his mind on the table games he and Jim and Yolanda played to pass the time. So he talked them into shooting some baskets. Usually Yolanda didn't like to do that. She was too small to get the ball high enough to go through the hoop. But Jim promised to help her. And she seemed a little nervous about her new parents being away, so she didn't want to stay in the house alone. They had played for only a few minutes when the phone rang. It was about five o'clock.

Daniel answered it, but it was his mother asking for Jim.

"Hi, Mom," Jim said. "No, I hadn't heard about it . . . Are you sure? It's clear here. Getting a little colder, but not much. We're outside now without even jackets on . . . Yeah, I understand . . . No, sure, I'll double check with Don. Listen, if he decides to go anyway, we'll probably go, so don't worry if you don't get an answer here . . . Yeah, well, OK. If you insist . . . No, I agree. See you . . . Bye."

By then Yolanda had joined Daniel in the living room.

"Bad news," Jim said. "Mom and Dad heard on the car radio about a freak spring storm that's headed our way. It should hit around eight o'clock. High winds, even snow, I guess. It already hit DePlatte."

9

"Are they coming home?"

"No, they're going the other way. It'll probably die down by the time it catches them."

"We can still go tonight, right?"

"I don't know. Mom wants me to make sure Don and Violet know about the storm. I'm to decide for myself whether we should go, no matter what they decide."

"You mean even if Don and Violet decide to try to make it on the bus, we might not go?"

"It's up to me, Dan. That's what Mom said."

"You'll let us go, right?"

"I don't know. I guess we'd be pretty safe on a bus. If Don is willing to risk it, I don't know why I shouldn't be. Still, it's a big responsibility. I'd never forgive myself if something happened to you two."

"Nothing would happen to us," Yolanda said. "You wouldn't let it."

"You got that right, Yo-Yo," he said. "Just to be safe, you'd better pack boots and winter coats and scarves and gloves while I'm calling Don."

Daniel and Yolanda lugged down extra duffel bags full of winter clothes. Jim reported that Don and Violet had already heard about the storm. They had decided to have everyone meet at the church, and they would make the final decision there.

"Will you go along with whatever Don says?" Daniel asked.

"Not necessarily. Of course, if he decides not to go, no one will go. But if he decides to go, I'm sure a few parents still won't send their kids. And I'm in charge of you two for the whole weekend. So I'll just have to decide then, too."

Daniel didn't think he liked that. He thought Jim wanted to go too. But it seemed that Jim was really worried about his responsibility. Daniel was glad that Jim took his job so seriously. But he hoped Jim would be willing to take a little risk so he and Yolanda could have their fun.

Anyway, the sky was clear. He jogged out to put the basketball and his bike away. He noticed that it was getting colder. But it was still bright outside. He just couldn't imagine a storm kicking up in that kind of weather. It certainly didn't smell like snow.

By the time they loaded up Jim's Camaro and pulled out of the driveway, Jim was serious and very quiet. That worried Daniel. There still were no clouds in sight. But for some reason, it did start to get dark earlier than any of them had expected.

At the church parking lot, several parents stood talking with Don and Violet. All the kids ran between the parked cars, laughing and playing. They had piled their bags into the bus and tried to forget that their parents and the leaders were gazing into the sky and listening to one of the car radios.

As darkness fell, the sky grew overcast and the temperature dropped again. Daniel didn't want to change into anything warmer, hoping to convince Jim that there was nothing to worry about. The kids quit running and playing when the Younglove family called their children—three too young for the outing and the two who were planning to go—back to their station wagon. They drove home.

Daniel was glum. He hoped no other parents would decide the same way. "I'm going to call the preacher," Don announced. "My feeling is that we should go. And if he says it's all right, I'll take whoever wants to come along."

The kids cheered and screamed, but the parents didn't look comfortable. When Don came back out of the church, a light snow appeared in the sky. He held out his open palm and looked up, squinting. "He says it's up to me. And I say I'm going to trust this big, high-riding bus. If we run into a storm, and it looks like we can't plow through, we'll turn back. Who's willing?"

Kids begged and pleaded with their parents all over the parking lot. Several parents insisted that Don call from the camp when they arrived.

"Can't do that," Don said. "No phone available there in the off season. But I'll call from the gas station down the road, and you can pass the word."

That satisfied everyone except a new couple who decided to take their daughter home. She looked relieved.

Jim was still staring at the sky and scowling. Finally he turned to Daniel and Yolanda. He motioned them closer.

"I'm sorry," he said. "But we're not going." .

2

The Plans Change Again

Daniel didn't even have time to get sympathy from his friends. They were piling onto the bus, whooping and hollering and climbing over the seats.

He wanted to plead with Jim. But his big brother had announced his decision with such finality that Daniel knew his mind was made up. Daniel just marched back to Jim's car and sat in the back seat, his arms folded. He stared at the floor. He was too mad even to cry.

When Jim and Yolanda reached the car, Yolanda was saying, "Can we really? That will be fun!"

"What?" Daniel demanded.

"Jim said he would stop at the library and get the video tape of *The Sound of Music*. And that we can stay up until nine-thirty and have popcorn while we watch it."

Daniel scowled and shook his head. "I'm sorry, Dan," Jim said. "I'm just doing what I think is best."

"It's not best for me!" Daniel shot back. "I've seen that dumb movie a million times."

Jim didn't answer.

At the library, Daniel stayed in the car while Jim and Yolanda went in to get the tape. Daniel couldn't figure out

13

why Yolanda seemed so happy. She probably hadn't wanted to go to the camp-out in the first place. She felt safer at home with Jim's full attention. Daniel couldn't remember when he had been so disappointed. And he resented Yolanda for not being as miserable at he was.

Worse yet, it stopped snowing before Jim and Yolanda returned to the car.

"Some snowstorm," Daniel muttered as Jim opened the door.

Jim looked up. "Hey, it did stop, didn't it?"

"Yes, it stopped! Let's hurry over to the church before the bus leaves!"

Jim hesitated a moment. "I don't think so, Dan."

"C'mon! Why not? You just don't want to go! You don't want me to have *any* fun!"

Jim didn't answer. He handed Daniel four books. Then he turned on the light inside the car so Daniel could see what they were. All were books about Daniel's favorite sports and athletes.

"I don't want to read," Daniel said. "I want to go to Camp Hickory."

"Well, we're not going," Jim said. "I may be wrong, but I have to stick with what I decided, all right?"

"No, it's not all right. Who wants to sit around reading books when all the other kids are out having fun?"

Jim turned on the news on the radio. "Apparently the snowstorm paralyzing the western part of the state will not reach us tonight, and is in fact giving signs of turning toward the south before dissipating."

"What does that mean?" Yolanda asked.

"I didn't understand all the words either, Yo-Yo," Daniel said. "But it sounds like we're not going to get the storm. Can't we go now, Jim?"

"Daniel, all he said is that the storm isn't going to hit our town. That camp-out is almost a hundred and fifty miles west, toward where the storm is. I'm not going to risk it."

Daniel grew stony and silent.

14

When they got home, two news bulletins came on television while Jim was trying to rig up the video player. Both said that the local area had escaped the danger of the big storm. But temperatures would be below normal for at least the next two days.

"Jim, for the last time, can't we go?"

Jim shook his head.

"At least call the church and see if they've left yet."

"Oh, I'm sure they have."

"You don't know that!"

"Why wouldn't they have left, Daniel?"

"Who knows?" He trudged upstairs to his bedroom and slammed the door. From below he heard Jim and Yolanda playing and laughing in the kitchen. He smelled the popcorn and the melted butter. Jim knew how to make good popcorn. But Daniel didn't want to admit he wanted any.

"Popcorn's ready, Dan!" Yolanda hollered up the stairs. "And Jim's starting the film!" He didn't answer. But he listened for the familiar music that signaled the start of what he had to admit was one of his favorite movies. He had seen it only twice all the way through and half of it another time. He hand't seen it for a couple of years, and, in a way, he really wanted to. But he was too mad at Jim.

He was hungry for popcorn, too. The smell was getting to him. It seemed as if it were right there in the room with him. He decided to sneak down and grab a bowl and eat it upstairs. As he opened the door, however, he realized why the smell had been so strong. Jim, or Yolanda, had left a huge bowl of popcorn, still hot, outside his door, along with the four books from the library.

Suddenly, he didn't want to be in his room, even though he didn't want to be with Jim and Yolanda either. He got a pillow and lay down in the hall with his books, slowly munching the popcorn. After a while, he felt lonely there, too. He was still mad at Jim, but he didn't want to be all by himself.

The popcorn was making him thirsty. So he took his

popcorn and his favorite book of the four down to the kitchen and poured himself a cold drink. Yolanda heard him rattling around out there. She came to investigate.

"Come on in with us, Dan," she said. "The good parts are coming up!"

He shook his head. "I want to go to the camp-out," he said, hoping she would tell Jim. She did. But Jim didn't say or do anything about it.

Eventually Daniel took his book and his popcorn and his drink down the hall and sat outside the family room. There he listened to the movie, reading and eating.

A couple of hours later, near the end of the movie, Jim came out, heading for the window at the end of the hall. He hesitated briefly as he saw Daniel. But he didn't say anything as he went by. He pulled the curtain back and looked at the sky. Then Daniel heard him at the front door. He felt the cold air snake its way through the house to where Daniel sat.

He couldn't deny that it was cold. Very cold. Way below freezing. But he was curious about what Jim was up to. Could he be changing his mind? Daniel wanted to help if Jim were undecided. He trotted to the front door.

"How's it look out there, Jim?" he asked kindly.

"Cold."

"I know. But it looks pretty clear, doesn't it?"

"Yeah. It does."

"Do you know how to get to Camp Hickory yourself, Jim? I know you've been there lots of times. In fact, you drove there once yourself, didn't you?"

"Twice."

"You thinking about trying to make it, Jim?"

"I shouldn't even consider it, the way you've been acting, Daniel."

"I know. I'm sorry."

"You should be. It's not easy having responsibility for two people besides myself. All you're thinking about is yourself and your fun. But I have to worry about the safety of you both."

16

"I know, Jim. I guess I was just so disappointed that it made me act mad."

"Well, it hurt me, Dan."

"I didn't mean to."

"It seemed like you *did* mean to. Your whole attitude was directed right at me because of the decision I made. I didn't appreciate it."

Daniel hung his head. "I'm sorry. I really am. If you don't want to try to make it to the camp or if you don't remember how to get there, I'll understand."

Jim shut the door and appeared to be thinking it over. "I'm not going to tell Mom or Dad how you've been acting, although I should. If you snap out of it now and don't do it again as long as they're away, I'll forget about it."

"Thanks."

"That doesn't mean I'm going to try to get to Camp Hickory tonight."

Daniel felt anger rising up in him again. And he realized that he had been sorry only because he thought he might persuade Jim to change his mind. He started to scowl and look down. But Jim's words were ringing in his ears. "I understand," he said, trying hard to sound as if he meant it. Down deep, he did. He knew Jim had a tough job, taking care of him and Yolanda. But he wanted to go so badly.

"I'm going to check the news one more time. Call the motor club number, Dan. You know, the one Dad had you call before they left."

Daniel ran to the phone. The recorded message said the roads were clear in a one hundred fifty mile radius from the city. There were bad conditions and even some road closings farther west. He ran to tell Jim, who had turned off the television and was giving instructions to Yolanda.

"Get all your stuff," he told both of them. "I'm going to call around and see if anyone has heard from Don Forester. If they made it, we'll head out."

3

Trouble

Daniel had all their extra things piled near the front door. Even Yolanda was starting to get excited about getting to go after all. She jumped and squealed right along with Daniel when Jim reported the good news from his phone call.

"They made it safe and sound," he said. "The weather is a lot colder there. But it's only snowing lightly. They won't be sleeping outside, but the program will go on as planned inside."

"Then we can go?" Daniel said.

"We can go," Jim said. He helped carry things to the car again. "We may not get there until midnight, but we'll get there. I know a little shortcut off the expressway, on a two-lane road through some farm country. That'll save us at least a half hour."

It took quite a while for the little car to warm up, but once it did, Daniel found it difficult to keep his eyes open. He buried himself under his woolly and furry parka and lay down in the back seat. Yolanda, meanwhile, was talking away with Jim.

About an hour into the trip on the interstate highway,

18

the snow began to fall more heavily. Daniel awoke to hear Yolanda telling Jim how beautiful it was. "Yeah," he said, "and it's not making the road slick either. We're still making good time."

Daniel peered out the back window. He saw two trucks, but no other vehicles on the road. It was toasty inside the car. But he could tell from the way the huge flakes were blowing past the light poles that it was bitterly cold outside.

He lay back down and tried to sleep. But he was too keyed up now. He sat up and stared out the front between Jim and Yolanda.

"We're making good time," Jim said again.

Daniel didn't respond. Far in the distance he saw brake lights. Two sets. Then three. Jim backed off the gas pedal a bit. When they caught up with the vehicles ahead they could see why everyone had slowed. The snow had begun to stick to the lightly traveled pavement. The roadway was slippery.

But not slippery enough to slow Jim. He picked his way through the slower cars and a truck and put some distance between himself and them. He was still traveling about forty-five miles an hour. The snow was covering the hood of the car, and the wipers were working hard to keep it off the glass.

The road was slushy, and the snow was heavier and deeper the farther they went.

"Should you slow down a little?" Daniel suggested.

"Nah. We're all right." But even as he said it, the Camaro began to fishtail. Luckily, there were no other cars nearby. Jim steered in the direction they were sliding. But the car made a full circle in the middle of the snow-covered road.

"Jim!" Yolanda squealed, and Daniel slammed up against the side window.

"We're all right," Jim said calmly as he continued to fight the wheel. The car went halfway around again and stopped, facing the wrong direction. "Hang on," he said. The cars more than a quarter mile behind slowed even more as they saw headlights pointed at them.

19

Jim turned the car around in the right direction and drove slower now. He reached over to put a hand on Yolanda's shoulder. "Sorry about that," he said. "Dan, you'd better get your safety belt on."

"Are we going to turn back, Jim?" Daniel asked, buckling up.

Jim shook his head. "I think we can make it. It's hard to tell how wide this storm front is. We may pull out of it. Anyway, we're only about forty miles from my shortcut. If it's clear at all, we'll be in good shape."

But within a half hour, they had gone only ten more miles. Jim had to keep reducing his speed as the winds blew against the car and made it sway. Ice and snow and slush caked on the left side windows. The wipers beat a pile of snow into a pack at the bottom of the windshield.

Jim had both hands on the wheel. He stared intently out into the swirling snow, lighted up by the headlights in the blackness. Even at slow speed, twice he had to fight to keep the Camaro from sliding out of control. They passed several cars that had either stalled or decided to wait out the worst of the storm.

"Good thing we started with a full tank of gas," Jim said.

"Should we stop and wait, too?" Yolanda asked.

"Not until the truckers start stopping. When they don't think they can go on, I sure won't either. Meanwhile, I don't think it's going to get any better. So we'd better keep pushing."

Yolanda wept softly. "I'm scared."

"Don't be, kid," Jim said. "I wouldn't let anything happen to you." And they moved on.

An hour and a half later, it was near midnight. They had made slow but steady progress. Jim thought the snow seemed to be letting up some. But it was still very cold. He went off the interstate onto a slippery ramp. Then he drove onto a road that had shallow drifts every few hundred feet.

He carefully wove through them. He was looking for

the shortcut road he remembered so well. "It seems like it should have been right around here somewhere," he said. "But it's been a long time, and we *are* going a lot slower than usual. Ah, there it is."

His headlights pointed to a road sign reading "Toboggan Road." "Look," he said. "It's clear because the snow fences are still up from last winter."

Indeed, the entrance to Toboggan Road was clear and even looked dry. Jim wasn't fooled by the appearance, however. He knew the now lightly falling snow could still cause a slick road. He carefully turned and was pleased with a clear, fairly dry road ahead for as far as he could see.

He turned on his bright lights, allowing him to look even farther. "All clear," he said, sighing in relief. "We still have to be careful. But I should be able to do about forty-five with no problem."

"That sounds too fast," Yolanda said.

"I'll do forty, if it makes you feel any better."

"Please."

"Me too," Daniel said.

"OK. Hey, I'll turn back and go home if that's what you two want."

"No, we want to keep going. How much farther is it?"

"Six miles on this road to Route Twelve, then west again about sixty miles to the camp. If we go forty miles an hour, how long will it take us, Dan?"

"Uh, let's see. An hour and a half, plus this road."

"Right!"

Daniel had just settled back in the seat and began to get drowsy again when Jim started pumping the brakes. The snowfall was heavier. The road was mushier. The visibility was shorter. "Shoot," Jim said, looking in the rearview mirror. "Look behind us, Dan."

Daniel looked out the back window. Every once in a while, during a slight break in the swirling snow, he could see the street light at the end of Toboggan Road. Snow was blowing all around it, even past the snow fences.

They had gone halfway down the road, and now there were no more snow fences. The weather had turned again. It looked as if their way out was quickly closing up.

"We'll just keep moving through for as long as I can see."

Daniel was as scared as Yolanda. But he didn't want to admit it.

Jim seemed mad. "Daniel," he said quickly, harshly, "you see why I didn't want to come?"

"Yeah, but—"

"Yeah, but nothing! You didn't want to listen to me. I told you it would be dangerous and that I shouldn't take the chance."

"So why did you change your mind?"

"Because you were acting like such a baby! That's why!"

Daniel was worried. He didn't want Jim to be upset when he needed to be driving carefully. He wanted to argue with Jim because now Jim was being unfair. Yes, Daniel had been acting difficult, but it had, after all, been Jim's decision to come.

"I'm sorry, Dan," Jim said. "I know I can't blame it on you. But this should be a lesson for all of us."

"It is," Daniel admitted.

Suddenly the wind was so strong and the snow so heavy that drifts formed in front of the car as they moved along. Jim picked his way through the deep snow.

"What's this?" he said. "I didn't remember that there were no streetlights in the middle of this road."

That's why it was so dark. There hadn't been a streetlight since the one at the entrance.

"I'm sure there's another at the other end," Jim said, "but who knows how far that is. If I can just keep an eye on the center line. There are no side lines on this road. And it looks like a pretty steep ditch."

Now they were just crawling along. "Any worse and I'll have to pull over for a while," Jim said.

"Please do," Yolanda said. "Please, Jim."

"But I don't want to get stranded here, Yo-Yo. If we get stranded anywhere, I'd rather it be on Twelve. Or back on the interstate. But we're not getting back there tonight."

"So we have to get to Route Twelve?" she asked, like a miniature news reporter.

Jim nodded, not taking his eyes from the road.

"Then that's what I'm going to be praying for," she announced. "And you'd better too, Dan."

Daniel closed his eyes. He wasn't praying they would reach Route Twelve. He was just praying they would be safe, no matter how far they got.

4
Stranded

Jim began fighting the wheel again. Both Daniel and Yolanda stiffened and glued their eyes to the road ahead. Or at least what they could see of it. Both thought they were spinning around again, but Jim knew better.

"Oh, no!" he said. "Not a flat! Not now!" But it was a flat. The car was weaving back and forth across the road, as if ignoring what Jim was doing with the steering wheel. He finally wrestled the car to the right side of the road onto the narrow shoulder.

He got out to have a look. Unfortunately the flat tire was the rear right. There would be nowhere for him to kneel to work on it. A steep incline shot down into a long, wide ditch on that side of the car.

Jim was wearing only a short windbreaker and no hat, scarf, or gloves. So he hurried back into the car. "Get my heavy stuff from the bag, Dan. I'm going to drive over to the other side and hope no one comes that way."

Daniel dug in his pile of stuff and found Jim's parka and stocking cap and scarf. The gloves were in the pockets of the parka. Jim slowly moved the car across the center of the road until he was half on the shoulder and half in the wrong lane on the other side.

"You two will have to get bundled up, too," he said, standing outside to pull on his coat. "You can't be in the car when I've got it up on the jack."

"Why not?" Yolanda said. "It's freezing out there!"

"Because if the weight shifts, the jack could slip. I don't need that. It's going to be almost impossible to change the tire in this weather anyway."

"Should we wait till it clears?" Daniel asked.

"I'd love to," Jim said. "But that might be morning. I'd rather be able to move a little, just to keep the car out of the snowdrifts. If the car gets surrounded, there's nowhere for the exhaust to go and the fumes get inside."

"That would keep us warm," Yolanda said. "Except it might stink."

"No, no!" Jim said. "Those fumes can kill you! You should be glad you can smell the stinky fumes. They can warn you of the poisonous ones. It's the fumes you can't smell, the carbon monoxide in the exhaust, that kills you. You don't even know what hits you. You might become a little sick to your stomach, or dizzy. But mostly you just get drowsy and fall asleep. Soon you're dead."

"You're kidding!"

"Hardly."

"How do you know so much about it?" Yolanda asked. She got out of the car, all bundled up against the snow. She stood with her gloved hands thrust deep into her pockets and her shoulders hunched to keep the wind off her neck.

"From chemistry class. The poison makes part of our blood unable to carry oxygen. And without oxygen, we're in trouble. Whenever you're in a place where there's car exhaust fumes, you have to make sure there's fresh air there, too."

Jim pulled the jack and lug wrench from the trunk. He squinted in the darkness. "Uh-oh," he said. "Dan, did you bring a flashlight?"

"No! Do you need one? The trunk has a light."

"Yeah, but I can't see the tire from that. I've go to have more light." They searched the whole car. Nothing. The only light they had came from the headlights and taillights.

"I guess I'll just have to do it by sense of touch," Jim said.

He yanked the spare tire from the trunk and slammed the lid shut. Rolling the tire to the side of the car, he laid it flat and sat on it. He felt for the wheel cover he would have to remove in the darkness.

"Should I turn the car off to save gas?" Daniel asked.

"I'd like to, but we need the lights on. They might drain the battery if the engine isn't running. Better leave it for now. If we get stranded, we'll only have it on when we absolutely need it for heat. We've got plenty of gas."

The wind kicked up. The snow fell more heavily. Jim and Daniel and Yolanda had to shout at each other to be heard. The ugly screeching of metal on metal as the wheel cover came loose was the only sound louder than the howling wind.

"Jim!" Daniel shouted. "Look!"

They looked ahead of the car, about a hundred feet. A four-foot drift had formed across the road.

"Put the brights on, Dan!"

Daniel sat behind the wheel and depressed the switch on the floor. The brights didn't help much. The beam just pointed higher into the air and was reflected back by the blizzard. It gave Jim a little more light on the flat tire, but no better clue of what was ahead.

"You two stand here and block the wind as much as you can, but stay about a foot apart so I get some of that light!"

It didn't work well. They blocked some wind. But the space they left for the light just sent the whistling snow all around Jim. He struggled and strained at the lug nuts. His fingers were icy even inside his gloves.

It felt to Jim as if he may have stripped the last nut with the lug wrench, but he just couldn't see. "I've got an idea," he

26

said. "You guys want to get back in the car and warm up a minute?"

Daniel said, Sure! But Yolanda was in the car almost before the word was out of his mouth. Jim followed close behind and sat in the driver's seat. He put on the emergency brake and put the car in reverse. That turned on the backup lights and would allow him a little better vision of the lug nuts. But the brake kept the car from moving.

"Stay here until I'm ready to jack it up. Then you have to get out."

Finally, Jim was successful. With all five nuts removed, he hurried back into the car for a break.

"Whew! That's cold!"

"Did you get it?"

"Yup. Just a matter of time now, and we can at least get on the other side of the road."

"Jim!" Yolanda squealed. "Do you see what I see?"

She was peering out the front window. What she could see, Daniel soon realized, was nothing. Nothing but white.

Jim turned the brights off. The normal headlight beamed confirmed his worst fears. Visibility was zero. They were in the middle of a full-fledged blizzard.

"Might as well wait till this clears at least," Daniel suggested.

"No way, Dan. I've got to get this car onto the other side of the road. Someone might be foolish enough to try to come through the other way."

"Who could make it?"

"A four-wheel-drive truck, or a snow plow. They'd never see us until it was too late to stop. I hate to say this, but you're going to have to get out with me."

"Oh," Yolanda moaned. "I'm scared."

"There's nothing to be scared of, Yo-Yo. As long as you stay close, and we get this tire changed so I can move the car. We've got lots of warm clothes and still plenty of gas, so we'll be all right. But we have to get out of the road."

They tumbled out and stayed together by holding hands

27

until Jim was back at his perch on the spare tire. Strangely, he had more light now that the snow had closed in around them. It served almost as a mirror, directing the light from the head and tail lights toward the flat.

He jacked the passenger side high enough to give him room to remove the tire.

But the blowing snow had covered the tire. It had even blown in around behind the wheel while they had been inside the car. The metal had been warm enough to melt the snow, but it had quickly refrozen. Now it was ice, and it held the wheel tight to the brake drum.

Jim pulled and pulled, but he couldn't pull the wheel off. So he began alternately pulling and pushing, even praying, hoping to break it free. Finally, be braced himself against the side of the car. He reached behind the tire and pushed with all his might.

Before he realized it, he was pushing the whole car back against the jack. He didn't know where the car would go if it slipped off the jack in all this snow. He also couldn't see where Daniel and Yolanda were standing!

5

The Injury

"Look out!" Jim screamed. He scrambled around to the rear of the car. Daniel and Yolanda stepped back as Jim braced himself against the rear of the car. The jack was tipping dangerously. In dry conditions, Jim could easily have pushed the car back to a safer position on the jack. But he was having trouble even staying on his feet in the snow.

"Get around beside the car," he ordered. "If that jack pops out, it could go flying. We don't want anyone to get hurt out here."

Daniel and Yolanda quickly obeyed.

"Be careful," Yolanda pleaded.

"Do you want me to help you push?" Daniel asked.

"Yeah," Jim said, "but I'm stuck."

The car had come down on him. But the brake drum was supporting the weight of the car. There was just enough weight on Jim to pin him but not to crush him.

"Pull the jack out, and jack this thing back up," Jim said to Daniel.

"I can't," he replied. "It's still hooked in the bumper." Jim looked over at where Daniel was struggling to pull the jack out. Sure enough, even though the car had pushed it over, it had not pulled free. The bumper was bent where the lip of the jack had pushed around farther than it should be. It was wedged in tightly.

"Now what?" asked Daniel.

"First we've got to cool off that exhaust pipe. It's already getting hot through my pants. You and Yo-Yo scoop some snow onto my right leg underneath here to cool off that pipe. Then I'll think of something."

Yolanda seemed relieved to have a job to do. But she was still crying. "I want us to get out of here!" she moaned.

"So do I," Jim said. "Don't worry. Keep praying that we'll get out." The snow on the hot pipe hissed and steamed. "Now Dan, get in and put the car in first gear. That's the farthest one to the right. Release the brake and try to pull ahead. But don't let it rock back, or it'll kill me."

"Oh!" Yolanda squealed. "Don't say that!"

"It's true, honey. I'm sorry. Can you handle it, Dan?"

"I don't know. Is there anything safer we can try?"

"No, I don't think so. I can't move. So we have to move the car. Just try to move forward a couple of inches, Dan. Then hit the brake so it doesn't slide back. OK?"

"I'll try."

"You can do it."

"I hope so."

"Dan! Stop being so negative! You have to do it. Yo-Yo's praying, and you concentrate. As soon as you move a little, I'll scramble out."

Daniel put the car in gear. It rolled forward, then started to slide to the left, off the shoulder. Daniel stopped, and the car rolled back.

"Ah!" Jim yelled. "Do that again and race it. And don't quit until you hear me!"

Daniel put the gas pedal to the floor, and Jim pushed with all his might. The car inched forward about a foot, and he dragged his legs out from underneath. As he scrambled to get to his feet, the car began to slide toward the ditch again.

30

The underside of the bumper scraped Jim's left leg just above the ankle. He was so cold and so eager to get free that he didn't notice any pain at first, until he tried to stand on both feet.

He began hopping and whimpering. The bumper had sliced through the skin. His leg was bleeding. He hopped to the front of the car, where Daniel was still racing the engine. Daniel looked up, shocked to see Jim. He let the car roll back. It lodged in the snowbank at the bottom of the ditch.

From the headlights, Jim got a good look at his wound. The gash was deep, into the tendons and muscle and partially through the bone. He knew he would be unable to help push the car. "At least it's out of the way of traffic."

"Traffic?" Daniel said. "There won't be any traffic through here for days."

"I hope you're wrong about that. Help me into the car."

"What are we going to do?" Yolanda said. "You're going to die if we don't get you to the hospital."

"Nah! I'll be all right, Yo-Yo. But I've got to sit down and get this foot up. Then we can figure out what to do."

"There's nothing to do!" she cried. "We're all going to freeze to death out here."

"Yolanda!" Jim shouted, grabbing her arm. "That's not going to help at all! We have to be calm and pray that God will help us."

"I already prayed, and He let the car run over you!"

"It's all my fault," Daniel muttered. "I made you come. None of this would have happened if I hadn't acted so badly."

"Will you two knock it off and get me in the car!"

The Camaro looked strange, its tail deep in the ditch, its headlights shining high into the sky across the road. All they could see in the light were the tumbling, darting flakes. it was so white that it seemed the three of them were walking around inside a Ping-Pong ball.

Daniel and Yolanda weren't much help. But Jim was able to crawl painfully into the back seat and rustle up

31

enough clothes to make a footstool. He propped his bad leg on it, and Daniel settled into the driver's seat. Yolanda sank into the other front seat.

"Now what?" Daniel said.

"Might as well turn the lights off," Jim said. "And the engine too. It's warm enough in here for now, and I don't want to open a window. Oh, no!"

"What?"

"My leg's bleeding more than I thought. We'd better freeze it."

"How?"

"Snow."

"How much?"

"As much as you can get. Is that wheel cover still in the road?"

Daniel turned the lights back on and got out. He returned with the wheel cover. "Who knows where the nuts are," he said.

"Never mind about those. Just fill that thing with snow and hand it to me."

When Daniel was back in the car, Jim had him turn on the inside light. Jim filled the scarf with snow, and as the snow started to slowly melt, he applied the compress directly to his gouged shin. He winced and hissed as the cold took hold. And he began to shiver. "I can't believe it's getting cold in here already," he said.

"Let me turn the engine on again, Jim," Daniel said. "I had the door open, and you've got snow on you and everything."

"Yeah, but then we have to open a window, unless you want to try digging out behind the car so the exhaust isn't blocked by the snowbank."

"I'll try," Daniel said. "You want to help, Yo-Yo?"

She shrugged but followed him out. He could see she was still crying.

6
Praying

Daniel felt his way to the back of the car. He talked gently to Yolanda the whole way. "Don't cry," he said. "We'll get out of this."

"How?" she said. "The snow's getting deeper, and I'm freezing!"

"We'll keep praying," he said. "Even if it keeps snowing, we have a car to sit in. And we shouldn't be hungry till morning. Then we can start on that bag of candy bars Mom packed. That'll keep us going for quite a while."

"That's right! There's a whole bag of them!"

"Sure!"

Daniel was on his knees, digging with both hands, feeling for the exhaust pipe. Finally, between the two of them, they had cleared about a three-foot scoop around it. The pipe itself was plugged with snow. "Let me ask Jim what to do about that," he said. In a minute, he was back.

"He says to dig it out as much as we can, then start the engine and be sure the snow blows out. If it doesn't, all that carbon whatever poison stuff comes right into the car. And then we'd have to sit there with the window open."

"That could be worse," she said.

Daniel found the lug wrench and poked it into the end of the exhaust pipe. But that just shoved the block of snow deeper. "Oh, no," he said. When he told his brother, Jim advised starting the car and gunning it. Yolanda would watch to see if the snow came out. Daniel was worried because Jim's teeth were chattering so much that he could hardly talk.

Daniel raced the engine for a few minutes. "All I saw in the red light back there," Yolanda said, "was a little smoke, then like water, then lots of smoke."

"That's good," Jim said, his lips blue. "Keep the windows shut and keep it running. That means you pushed the snow so far in that it melted. We should be OK, as long as the drifts don't fill in behind the car again. You'll have to keep checking on that."

Yolanda crawled over Jim and found a blanket and a couple of sweaters, which she placed around Jim to try to keep him warm.

"Thanks, Yo-Yo," he said.

"Jim, are you going to sleep, or what?" Daniel asked. "If you want me to do something, tell me now. Or are we just going to wait out the storm?"

"I think we should try that first," Jim said. "Right now I don't know what else to do."

"I could try walking to a gas station or something," Daniel said.

Jim waved at him and shook his head. "No way," he said. "Too far, and you can't see. Snow's too deep." He seemed to be drowsy.

"What're we going to do?" Yolanda asked.

"Pray," Daniel said. And he closed his eyes. She did the same. Jim had fallen asleep.

While Jim slept, Daniel turned on the inside light again and tried to get a better look at Jim's leg. The bleeding had stopped but most of the snow had melted. If it had been the cold snow that had stopped the bleeding, Daniel knew that as the car warmed up the bleeding might start again. He turned off the engine and curled up in the seat. The windows were fogged up from the inside. Ice was forming on the windshield. Worst of all, it was still snowing.

In half an hour, Yolanda seemed to be sleeping. Daniel couldn't. He wanted to do something besides just sitting there waiting for the storm to break. Jim was right, he knew. He couldn't go out trying to walk somewhere, at least not until the weather broke.

He turned the ignition key to the position labeled "ACC." Then he tried to tune in his favorite radio station. All he got was static. He searched the dial for any station he could find. On one end he heard music, faintly, as if from far away. At the other end, he could make out some news.

"Every major thoroughfare in the western part of the state is closed," the voice said. "And there appears to be no break in the storm. Not even snowplow operators can get out to come to work. If you're stranded, remember, be sure your exhaust system is clear of snow and that you keep a window open when the car is running. To conserve gasoline, run the engine only about five minutes every half hour. Don't leave your car! Stay where you are. Someone will find you at daybreak. If your car is buried, try to uncover enough of it so emergency vehicles can see you in the morning."

Daniel turned on the engine and looked at the clock. One-thirty in the morning. He let it run five minutes. The inside heated up. Jim was still, but it seemed he was having trouble breathing. Yolanda appeared to be sleeping except that she was rocking back and forth.

There was still a quarter tank of gas. Daniel didn't know how long that would last. Maybe quite a while if they could really get along on just five minutes every half hour. But already the car was getting cold again. He wondered how early the sun would rise. He wondered whether the storm would have let up enough by then so that he could even see the sun.

Suddenly, Jim was awake and sounded worried. "We

35

have to make sure I don't go into shock," he said. "I feel cold and clammy, and my heart is beating strangely."

"What's shock?" Daniel asked. "And what do I do?"

Yolanda began praying aloud.

"I'm not entirely sure myself," Jim said, "but I think I have to loosen my clothes and keep my head lower than my feet. But that's going to be hard in this little car. Help me get my foot up on the dashboard."

Jim put both feet out in front of him and then crossed his legs at the ankles, the wounded shin on top of the other. Daniel carefully cupped his hands under Jim's ankles and helped him get his heels on the dashboard and his back flat on the back seat. Jim was awkward and uncomfortable with the back of his head pressed against the back of the seat. "I won't be able to sit this way long," he said. "But I do feel better already."

He unzipped his parka and unfastened the top two buttons of his shirt. "I'm hungry," he said. "Where are those candy bars?"

"Right here," Yolanda said. "But don't you think we should make them last? They might be our only food for a couple of days."

"A couple of days? I hate to tell you, Yo-Yo, but I'm not going to last a couple of days."

"Don't say that, Jim!"

"I'm sorry, Yolanda. But I have to get this leg treated or I'm going to be in big trouble. We don't have enough gas to keep me warm all the time, and I have to guard against hypothermia."

"What in the world is that?"

"That's when the body temperature starts falling, and you can't retain heat. If you get down something like four degrees from normal, you can die. Any lower, and you're sure to."

"You think a candy bar will help that?"

"Can't hurt. It'll start my digestive juices and get some sugar to my brain. If nothing else, I should be able to think."

She unwrapped a candy bar and handed it to him.

"How many are left?" he asked.

She counted them. "Twenty-one."

"We can each have four tomorrow if we're still stuck here. That'll leave three for each of us the next day."

"You'll need more than we will," Daniel said. "Because you're bigger, and you're hurt."

"Look on the bright side," Jim said. "I might not last till the second day. Then you two can fight over the ninth candy bar, after you've each had four."

"That's not even funny," Daniel said.

"I know. I'm sorry. Don't worry, I'll make it."

"I wish you hadn't said that," Yolanda said, crying again.

"That I would make it? Thanks a lot, Yo-Yo!"

"No! The other! Oh, *you* know what I mean! Don't say anything more about dying, OK?"

"OK," he said, smiling, his mouth full. "I hope this doesn't make you hungry, but I need it."

"It does," Daniel said. "It makes me want one."

"Me too," Yolanda said. "But we have to save them. If we were home we'd be sleeping right now."

"That's what you ought to be doing," Jim said. "But Daniel, keep an ear out for a snowplow or a grader or even a tractor. Anything. If something comes by, get those lights on, even if you don't have time to start the car. Got it?"

"Got it."

Jim sat up again, carefully pulling his feet back down to his makeshift footstool. He looked and sounded better. The candy bar had done the trick, at least for now. "Hey," he said, "is it just my imagination, or has the snow stopped?"

Daniel pulled the lights on briefly. The wind was still raging, but the snow in the air was from the ground and the drifts. It had stopped snowing.

7

Taking the Risk

"If it doesn't snow till daybreak," Jim said, "someone is sure to find us then."

"But what if they don't?" Yolanda asked.

"With you praying, how can they help it?"

"But what if they don't?" she persisted.

"Then I'll head out," Daniel said. He expected Jim to protest, but Jim didn't.

Jim nodded. "You may have to," he said. "If it's clear, if you can see, if we can find you enough warm, dry clothes. We'll have to try to decide which is closer, the interstate or Route Twelve."

"Which do you think?" Daniel asked. He was not sure he was quite as brave now as he'd thought he was.

"Twelve," Jim said. "At least maybe you can flag down a truck or a plow or something or find a house with a phone. Just in case, you'd better get some sleep."

That was easier said than done. "I'm too cold to sleep," Daniel said.

"Think about the candy bar you'll get for breakfast," Jim said.

"And the ones you'll take with you," Yolanda added.

"I hope I don't have to go anywhere," Daniel said.

"So do I," Jim said. "Let's hope and pray that we'll be found at dawn."

"I've been praying all night, Jim," Yolanda said. "I wish you'd pray aloud the way Mom and Dad do."

Jim looked at her. "I will if you want me to." Daniel nodded. "Dear Father in heaven," Jim began. "We love You because You love us. We know You know where we are and why we're here. We pray we would learn whatever lessons You have for us, because we know You allowed this for a purpose. May it make us less selfish. May it make us wiser and more careful. May it bring us closer to each other and make us learn to rely on You more. Forgive us for what we've done wrong. Help us do whatever we have to. We need Your help, and we want to be safe and warm and get out of this mess. In Jesus' name, amen."

It was snowing lightly when the first pink light of morning swept across the sky.

Jim stirred. "Start the engine, Dan, and let her run for fifteen minutes."

"Are you sure?"

" 'Fraid so. I wouldn't be surprised if my body temperature is down, and I can't afford that."

Jim passed out candy bars, and they all ate eagerly.

"Slow down," he cautioned. "There are some good things for you in a candy bar. But there are also things that make you hungrier and upset your stomach. You'll get instant energy, and maybe the two of you should get out and stretch a little. You're going to have to help me out and stand for a few minutes in a while anyway."

"We are?" Yolanda said.

"Sorry, yes. I need to move around a little to keep the blood circulating."

"How's the leg?"

"You don't want to know."

"Yes, I do!"

"It hurts."

Daniel and Yolanda discovered that drifts had filled the underside of the car with snow. The only melted spot was where the muffler had been running for the last few minutes. The tail pipe was still clear. But the car was in the ditch to stay—at least until a wrecker pulled it out. Daniel had been having a harder and harder time starting it every half hour. At least he hadn't used much gas.

Because of the contour of the land, the Bradfords couldn't see either end of the road they were on, even when the snow stopped and the sky cleared a bit. "I wonder if there's any reason for a car or truck or anything to come down this road today," Jim said.

"Only as an answer to my prayer," Yolanda said.

They helped Jim out of the car. It was a slow, painful ordeal for him. Daniel and Yolanda strained to keep him from falling. He winced and groaned, but he kept saying he was all right and that it was good for him.

To Daniel, he looked pale and weak, and Daniel asked him if he wanted another candy bar. "Yes, but I'd better save them," he said.

"You think Mom and Dad know we're stranded yet?" Daniel asked.

"I doubt it. If they called home, they probably assumed we went on the campout. Unless they somehow heard that Don and Violet and the gang made it without us, how could they know? There's no phone working at the camp either."

"How about the person you talked to who had heard from Don?"

"I told him we were going. Unless he talks to Don and finds out we never made it, no one will even be worried about us or looking for us."

"Then who'll find us?" Yolanda asked.

"I don't know," Jim said, his hand on her shoulder. "If no one finds *us* we may have to find *them*."

"We're a long way from Camp Hickory."

"I know, but we've got to find somebody."

40

"When?"

"Let's give it one more hour. If no one tries to clear this road then, Dan, you're going to have to see how far you can get."

"And what if I can't get through?"

"Then you come back here with us, and we'll hope for the best."

"Hope nothing," Daniel said, helping Jim back into the car. "If I have to come back, we're all going to die here."

"Good grief, Dan, have you lost faith already? We've got enough shelter and candy bars to keep us going for several days. These freak storms never last more than a day or two. It'll melt as fast as it came. We can all walk, or at least hobble, out of here."

Daniel glared at his brother in the cozy car he was so tired of already. "You know as well as I do that we can't wait for the weather to clear. If you don't get someone to treat your leg, you could die. I should be out there right now."

Jim sighed. He wasn't smiling. "Dan," he said, his voice weak. "I admit I'm glad to hear you say that. The last thing in the world I want to do is to send you out in this weather. But you're right. I'm no help, and I do need a doctor. I'm afraid we have no choice. When you're ready, I'll tell you what to wear, what to watch out for, and where to go."

Daniel turned and faced the windshield. He turned on the defroster and watched the ice slowly melt from the inside of the windshield. It was cold and gray out, but the snow had stopped again. They listened to the radio and heard the bad news. More snow was expected. Not much. Not like before. But some. And no one knew quite when.

"I'm going now," Daniel said. "So tell me what to do."

Jim lurched around until he was sitting forward, leaning over his legs, wound and all. "Start with your feet," he said. "They're the most important. Then your hands. Then your head and face. Everything else should take care of itself because of the body heat you will generate by walking."

"What do you mean, start with my feet?"

"Let me see your boots." Daniel lifted his foot to show Jim his cowboy boots. "Oh, no," Jim said. "Are those all you have?"

"Except for my sneakers."

Jim shook his head.

"What's wrong, Jim? They're warm enough."

"Not for a three-and-a-half mile hike through this, they're not. You have to have at least three pairs of socks on, a light one, then two heavy ones. You'll never get those things on over that."

"I know. I can't even get these on over one pair of sweat socks. But they'll keep me dry."

"No, forget it, Daniel. Trust me. You'll get frostbitten toes, and you'll be no good to us."

"I have good, lined boots," Yolanda said. "See?"

"You're right," Jim said. "They're perfect. But there's no way you're going out there."

"You're telling me," she said. "I sure wouldn't want to go alone."

"I don't either," Daniel said. "But I'm willing to take the risk."

"Well don't make it sound like I don't care!" Yo-Yo said. "I would if I had to."

"Hey, you two. Knock it off," Jim said.

Yo-Yo was starting to cry again. "I'm sorry," Daniel said. "I didn't mean it that way."

"All right, Dan," Jim said. "Get your boots off and start putting the socks on."

"What am I going to wear?"

"*My* boots."

"Yours?! You wear a thirteen and a half!"

"Got any better ideas?"

Daniel took his boots off. When he had three pairs of socks on, Jim had him put a pair of corduroy pants over his jeans. Then he layered on several pullover shirts and one of Jim's big flannel ones. Then a sweater. Then a windbreaker. Then his big coat.

"A ski mask and a stocking cap both," Jim advised. By now Daniel looked like a snowman, or a kindergartner going off to his first winter day of school. "After you get my boots on, put on your gloves with fingers, then my big mittens," Jim said.

"You'd think I was going to the North Pole," Daniel said from somewhere deep inside his wraps.

"You're going to feel as if you have," Jim said.

8

On Toboggan Road

Daniel pulled on Jim's huge boots that came nearly up to his knees. They were fur-lined and thick, with giant soles and deep treads. He knew he would feel and walk like a clown. He also knew he would be protected from the cold.

Daniel listened intently as Jim ran down a list of warnings and tips. "Always look for the lowest ground. At first you'll feel like you can climb through any drift, but that's work. You'll soon be exhausted. Try to stay out of the ditch, because if you come to a drift in there, you'll have to climb up to the road again. Just look for spots where the snow isn't so deep. It's still going to wear you out. But you can go longer if you find the easiest way."

Jim reached over to unzip Daniel's parka pocket. He stuffed two frozen candy bars inside.

"Two?" Daniel asked.

Jim nodded. "I hope you don't need more. You should eat the first one around one o'clock. You really need to wait that long if you can. Save the other until you find someone.

"Who?"

"I don't know, but that's the whole point. You walk until

you come to Route Twelve. Unless you find someone plowing through Toboggan Road. On Twelve you go left. I don't remember how far it is to the first farmhouse or gas station. And I don't know which you'll come to first, either."

"Or even whether Twelve is open."

"Right."

"So I'm just looking for anybody?"

"Absolutely. Anyone who is out walking, driving, whatever. Get them here to get us out, or have them call someone to rescue us."

"What if they won't come?"

"They'll come. The only reason anyone would be out this morning would be to help people. We'll be praying for you, Daniel. Be smart. If you need to slow down and rest, do it. If you can't get through, come back."

"Then what will we do?"

"I don't know. I haven't thought that far ahead yet."

"How's your leg?"

"Not too good. It's stiff and sore. I can tell there's some real damage there. I'm just hoping I'm better by basketball season next fall. If I'm not, it could change my whole life. How soon I get help will make a difference, Dan."

"I'm going."

It was eight-thirty Friday morning when Daniel left the car. The exhaust was sending a cloud of steam from the snowbank in the ditch, but the windshield was heavily fogged over. "Be careful, Daniel," Yolanda called as he slammed the door.

He worried about Jim because he didn't look well. He was pale, and he was shivering. Of course, they all were. But Daniel guessed that Jim hadn't slept much, if at all.

Daniel felt weird with Jim's gigantic boots on. He had to spread his feet wide to climb up out of the ditch. But the first fifty feet or so of Toboggan Road were covered with only about a foot of snow.

By lifting his feet high on every step, he was able to make his way through it. His eyes and mouth were cold already from the frigid wind that seeped through his ski mask. He pulled his scarf up over his mouth and nose. Now he was just peeking out over the top. That made him stumble because he couldn't see to balance well.

Then he came to his first drift. It was high, more than four feet in spots. He turned to look back at the car. Amazing. He knew he wasn't far from it, but he couldn't see it. Not at all. If he stopped and listened carefully, he could hear it running, but he couldn't see the exhaust. Couldn't see anything.

The drift looked most shallow on the far left and right. He headed left. Wasn't that what Jim had said? Find the shallowest part? Right. But he also said to stay out of the ditch. Which is what Daniel found himself in as he tried to walk through the drift. No wonder it was shallower!

First he was in up to his knees. As he lifted his legs higher and higher, he stumbled deeper into the ditch at the bottom of the drift. He kept on his feet, however, and was able to turn around and push his way back to the road. Apparently the only way through the drift was straight ahead.

He climbed the drift and found it both hard and soft. It was hard enough when he was climbing up that he could get atop it on all fours. But as soon as he started crawling, it was soft enough to let him sink in. From the top he could see that it was only about ten feet long, so he took a deep breath, thought about his brother and sister back in the car, and scrambled to the other side.

He fell and rolled down the front of the drift to shallow, powdery snow on the other side. On either side of the road, he saw fencing. The bottoms of the poles and lower lines of the wire mesh were buried in snow.

As Daniel staggered along, he realized he was heating up. Sweating. Puffing. His face was still cold. And he could feel the icy temperature in his thighs and in his neck. But he was steaming everywhere else. He was tempted to take his coat off, but then he would have to carry it.

46

He also knew he would freeze if he let the wind get at the moisture on his body. He was tired from lack of sleep, from huffing and puffing, and from being scared. He kept pushing on, walking in that funny way he had to because of the boots.

To take his mind off how far it was and how slow he was going, he tried humming songs to the rhythm of his feet. But he was going so slow that that didn't help. He tried singing to himself, then talking. He told himself stories. He encouraged himself. He prayed out loud.

If only the wind would slow down a little, maybe he could see how far it was to Route Twelve. He felt as if he'd gone about a half mile. It had taken him at least twenty-five minutes. At that rate, he was getting nowhere fast.

Daniel began feeling guilty and sorry for himself. Why had he coaxed Jim to come? Why had he been so mean and nasty? Why couldn't he just trust his big brother? On the other hand, why didn't Jim come in the first place so they could have beaten this storm?

He wondered where his parents were. He wondered whether they had any idea where Jim and Yolanda and he were. Especially Daniel. Could they imagine that everything had all been left up to him? In a way, that made him proud.

But what was he going to do if he ran out of energy? That candy bar seemed awfully good right then, but he knew he couldn't have it. He had to keep plowing on and some-how make it to Route Twelve.

In the next hour, he climbed over four drifts. He stum-bled and fell three times, once hard enough to roll over twice. He slipped down into the ditch once. But he kept bouncing up and keeping on. He got into a little rhythm and felt as if he were stronger and looser and was making better time. He thought he had to be getting somewhere close to Route Twelve. But he figured if he was going on a mile every half hour or so, it would take him another hour and a half at the very least.

Just thinking about that made him tired. He wanted to

sit and rest. But where could he sit without getting cold? He had to keep moving, keep moving, keep moving. He hoped the sun would break the cold some, but he couldn't even see the sun.

Soon Daniel came upon an unexpected bonus. It was something Jim hadn't remembered, or at least hadn't told him about. There was a steep hill, heading down. Daniel started walking faster and faster. Soon he was jogging, trotting, running full-speed, then out of control. He was almost flying down the hill!

His big, floppy boots were flailing away behind him. He could hardly keep his balance. Just as he was about to tumble headlong onto his stomach, the road leveled out and he was able to stay up. It was a good thing, because at the bottom of the hill was a drift that would take him five minutes to climb through. If he'd have hit that head-on at full speed, he might have buried himself for good.

When he got out of the other side, gasping for breath, he couldn't believe his eyes. There was a break in the wind, and he could see ahead. The hill went back up again, steeper than the one he had come down.

Was this the way it was going to be now, Daniel wondered, all the way to Route Twelve? Up and down, up and down? He prayed it wouldn't be. He wanted to get to the top of that hill and wait for another break in the wind to discover whether he could see all the way to Route Twelve. He just had to know how far he was from there.

But he didn't know whether he could make it.

9

Snow Plow!

It was after ten-thirty in the morning when Daniel reached the top of the hill. The wind was still blowing so that he couldn't see anything. If it would break for a minute, he could see all the way to Route Twelve. He just knew it.

His legs were aching. So he sat on the side of the road, his knees tucked up under his chin and his arms wrapped around his shins. Within a few minutes, he was so cold he could hardly move. He stood and thought about moving carefully down the other side of the hill. But the wind hadn't died down yet. And he had no idea what kind of progress he had made or how far he was from his goal: Route Twelve. He decided to wait five more minutes. He was glad he did.

For a few minutes, the wind slowed. It didn't die. But the snow blowing around was just a wispy mist. And the sun even tried to peek through. Far, far, in the distance—Daniel guessed about a mile—he saw a row of telephone poles crossing Toboggan Road. That could mean only one thing. Route Twelve.

He wondered at first if it wasn't his imagination. He squinted in the blinding whiteness and kept staring. Waves

49

of snow blocked his vision and then cleared, then blocked, then cleared. Yes, they were telephone poles. But if that was Route Twelve, it was closed, too. He didn't see or hear any traffic either way.

But there was something else, something at the corner of Route Twelve and Toboggan. What was it? He couldn't make it out. It looked black, like a big box with something on the end of it. But soon the sun was hidden, and the wind kicked up again. If he wanted to know what was there, he'd have to walk to it.

There was only one smaller hill between him and the intersection—and a few drifts to fight through.

Daniel figured it would take him another hour to get there. He was almost right. An hour and ten minutes later, he high-stepped through the last drift and could see the intersection. The sign said it was Route Twelve.

He was stiff-legged and bone weary. He didn't know how much closer he was to a car or truck or a person or a phone. But he felt good that he had accomplished something. He had walked more than three miles. He had reached the road Jim had told him about.

It was almost time to eat his candy bar. He switched it from his parka pocket to one of his shirt pockets so his body heat would thaw it. It was as hard as a brick.

He didn't know whether he wanted to walk down the middle of a busy road or not. But of course it didn't make any difference on a day like this. Then he saw it, the big black box he had seen from the top of the hill a mile away. It wasn't a box at all. It was a four-wheel-drive truck with a snow blade on the front. It was on its side in the ditch on the other side of Route Twelve at the corner. Route Twelve was covered with snow about two feet deep.

Daniel fought his way to the truck, which also snow-covered. "Hey!" he hollered. He was surprised at the sound of his own voice in the stillness. The wind stopped, and it was deathly silent. He wondered if this was what it was like at the North or South Pole. All white, all snow, no sound.

There was no answer. He wasn't tall enough to see in the door because of the truck's being on its side. So he climbed through the snow and over the blade, onto the door. He cleared way the snow from the windshield. No one was inside. The engine was cold.

There were no tracks, either of tires or boots. That meant that this accident had to have happened early in the blizzard. It had happened early enough for the people to escape and probably get help, but late enough that it had been impossible to get back and pull the truck out.

Daniel swung his legs out over the side and let his feet dangle. It felt so good to rest a minute. He pretended that a house or gas station would be just up the road. He knew that if he had to go as far as he had already come, he would panic. He wouldn't be able to make it.

He stood up on the truck to look out of the ditch and down Route Twelve. What a break! Because of crosswinds, there seemed to be no drifts on the road. Jut that two-foot pile for as far as he could see. It would be hard walking through that, but that was better than the deeper drifts.

He leaned back against the snow blade and sighed. He needed to get a little rest and maybe try that candy bar now. If it was thawed enough, it would give him energy for the next part of the journey—the part that Daniel hoped would be the last.

Ooh, it was cold. Daniel might have dozed otherwise. He shut his eyes and hung his head. It seemed in spite of the heat deep within the parka, he had a chill that went to his bones. He felt for the candy bar. It was soft. At least softer. He ripped it open and gobbled it. He knew he should eat it slowly, but he couldn't.

Within minutes he had a surge of energy, but also hunger that drove him on. As he struggled to his feet, he slipped off the side of the truck and fell headfirst into the snow. He was unhurt but felt stupid. Worst of all, now he heard something, a rumble.

He turned around quickly, but the sound wasn't in the

51

ditch. It was up on the road. And it was loud! What was it? He tried to scramble up the side of the ditch, but he couldn't get any traction. It sounded like a train! He had to get up there!

He jumped up on the side of the truck again and tried to stand, but he slipped again. As he was spinning and falling off, he caught sight of the noisemaker. A snow plow! One of those huge, ten-foot high double bladers coming right down the center of Route Twelve, throwing snow off both sides.

"Hey!" Daniel shouted, waving from the ditch. "Hey! Hey! Over here!" But the shower of snow that covered him and the truck in the ditch proved that he was neither seen nor heard. His heart was racing, and he was desperate. He used those big clodhoppers of Jim's to propel him out of the ditch. He ran down the road after the snow plow.

What a relief not to have to march through deep snow for the first time in hours. He ran and ran, hoping the driver would notice him out of his rearview mirror. But there was such a blizzard created by the plows that the driver couldn't have seen anything behind him.

Daniel slowed and stopped. He prayed the plow would come back. Even with the double blade, he had really cleared only about a lane and a half right down the middle. And didn't those plows usually come in twos? He searched the horizon behind him for another. Nothing.

The run had left him drained and freezing. He needed shelter. What was that Jim had warned him about? Hypothermia? He didn't feel as if his temperature had gone down. But he was shivering and he needed a break from the wind and cold. The only answer was the truck in the ditch.

He slowly headed back to it. He hoped a plow would come by before he got there so he could find shelter in a warm truck with a driver he could talk to. No such luck. He got back to the small truck and tried to open the door that was sticking up from the right side. It wouldn't budge. Apparently, it was locked.

He looked through the window again and saw a citizens' band radio. If that worked, he might not have to walk any more at all! He looked around for something he could use to break the window. He couldn't pull the wheel covers off without a tool. Anything else handy was probably buried in the snow.

He kicked at the ground, angry. Why couldn't there be something around that would break that window? With the bottom of the truck facing him, he saw the exhaust system with the long tail pipe. *I'll bet I can break that off,* he decided.

He pulled at the far end until the pipe bent at the first joint. Then he pushed and pulled until the joint gave way and a section about three feet long broke loose. Daniel climbed up on the side of the truck again and began whaling away at the window. But it was too strong. Either because of the cold or just its thickness, he couldn't get through it by swinging at it.

He hoped that driving straight down on it, as he would if he were digging a fence-post hole, might do the trick. It did. He succeeded in punching a hole through the window large enough to get his hand in and unlock the door. But still it wouldn't open. Frozen.

Angrily, he stuck the pipe back into the hole and began digging out large sections of window. The glass was held together with a gummy plastic used to keep it from shattering. But even that was brittle in the icy winds. Finally, he had removed the entire window and was able to swing his feet down into the front seat.

He wound up standing on the driver's-side door. It was almost impossible to squat in there to work the radio. With some effort, he hunched himself down and turned the switch on.

10
Success?

No sound came from the radio. And the little green light did not come on. Daniel knew then that the radio would work only if the engine was running. There were no keys in the ignition. Could he get it to run by doing something under the hood. Was there a way to connect the radio directly to the battery? He had no idea, and he wasn't about to try.

Meanwhile, Daniel felt warmer than he had for hours. He wasn't comfortable, all scrunched up down there, but, for a few minutes at least, it was better than being out in the snow.

Something was nagging at his mind. He finally realized what it was. He knew he should be grateful for the fact that Route Twelve had been plowed from the direction he was headed. He prayed and thanked God that the next part of the trip wouldn't be so difficult. But still, he had no idea what he'd find.

Climbing back out of that truck was harder than Daniel imagined. He still couldn't push the door open. So he had to put his foot on the steering wheel. He pushed himself up to where he could get his head and chest out the window, rest his hands on the door, and pull himself straight up.

Up on the road, he moved along briskly. He knew that would keep him warm longer. He seemed to be moving more than twice as fast as before because now his boots were almost touching the pavement. The only snow between his soles and the road was tightly packed and easy to walk on.

He came around a bend after passing nothing but trees and fields. And he saw a gas-station sign far in the distance! It was one of those high signs that can be seen for miles. So he couldn't tell exactly how far away it was. But he knew if he could get to it, even if it was closed, he could call someone.

But suddenly, from behind him, he heard something. He turned around and saw it was a snow plow. The same one? He didn't know or care. This time he would stand right in front of it if he had to. If it was obvious the driver couldn't see him, he'd leap out of the way at the last instant. But he just had to get the man's attention this time.

Something was different this time though. It didn't have the same rumble as before. He peered down the road and noticed that the blade was up, not scraping the snow. Good. That would make it easier. It wouldn't be so noisy. And there wouldn't be flying snow to block the driver's vision.

The plow was still not even up to Toboggan Road yet. Daniel moved out into the middle of Route Twelve and prepared to wave his arms over his head. But the snow plow slowed at the corner of Twelve and Toboggan. *I wonder if he saw the four-wheel-drive truck stuck in the ditch,* Daniel thought.

But no! The driver lowered the blade, and a wrenching, scraping sound quickly reached Daniel's ears. The plow was turning onto Toboggan! Jim and Yolanda would be saved! Daniel ran back as fast as he could, forgetting the cold, forgetting his stiffness, forgetting his hunger, forgetting his exhaustion.

He almost even forgot the big floppy boots he was

wearing. They were the only things slowing him down. He wondered if he could catch that plow. He ran and ran. But by the time he reached Toboggan Road again, the plow was almost out of sight. All he could see from the corner was a cloud of swirling snow as the plow went up and down the hills it had taken him so long to climb.

If only he had stayed with Jim and Yolanda! He wouldn't have had to do all this walking! But he didn't care now. As long as they were safe and someone could get Jim to a hospital, that was all that mattered.

There was no way they could have known a snow plow would come by. So Daniel had had to do what he had done. And he felt good about that. He couldn't run anymore, and he didn't know how long it would take him to walk the three-plus miles back to the car. He wanted to be there soon after the plow got there so they wouldn't have to come looking for him.

Jim would probably figure that Daniel had already gotten much farther. He wouldn't think to send the plow back looking for him. Daniel just hoped that the plow wouldn't take Jim the other direction to the hospital. Then it would be even later in the day before Daniel would be picked up.

He hurried along, running when he could and walking fast the rest of the time. An hour later, he chugged up the last big hill, his lungs aching and his whole body screaming for rest. He looked down to where he remembered the car being in the ditch, but he couldn't see it.

Surely there hadn't been time for the plow to go get a wrecker. Unless he had a radio. Maybe that was it. The snow-plow driver had radioed ahead for a wrecker and an ambulance. Or maybe he took Jim to the hospital himself. Now what should Daniel do? He didn't know.

He eased down the other side of the hill and slowly ambled toward the frontage road on the other end of Toboggan Road. They had to have gone that way. But when he got to where the car should have been, he saw no tracks, no sign of a wrecker or an ambulance, or even of the snow plow's stopping.

The low, muffled sound of a car horn came from deep in the ditch under a huge pile of snow. It couldn't be! The plow couldn't have buried the Camaro! Daniel dove into the snow, yelling for Jim and Yolanda. He dug as fast as he could with his hands.

The snow wasn't tightly packed. But it was obviously too heavy around the doors for his brother and sister to get them open. He hoped enough air was getting through. He knew some was, because somebody was honking that horn. "I'm coming, Jim!" he screamed. "I'm coming, Yo-Yo!"

"Oh, Daniel," Jim said as he broke through and could see them through the window. "Daniel, God answered our prayer!"

Daniel told them what had happened to him. And Jim told what had happened to them. "Snow plow. He rumbled past, but we had the car running and didn't hear him until he was right over us. Otherwise Yolanda would have run out to flag him down."

"She would have been killed!" Daniel said. "He can't see anything with all that snow flying around. How do I get these doors open, Jim? There's a ton of snow around the car."

"Never mind the doors for now. Get the car clear from behind so we can start the engine again. As soon as the plow went by I had to shut it off."

Jim looked terrible. Both he and Yolanda were white from the scare, and Yolanda wasn't saying anything. "You all right, Yo-Yo?" Daniel asked through the window. She just nodded and buried her head in Jim's arm.

"I need some more snow for the wound, too, Dan," Jim said.

It was half an hour before Daniel had cleared enough snow from behind the car that they could turn it on and get some heat inside. Daniel scooped snow through the window so Jim could fill the scarf he was applying to his leg. Then he dug out Yolanda's door so she could help him dig the other side.

"Jim's going to die in there," Yolanda moaned.

"Don't say that, Yo-Yo. God's been taking care of us so far."

"How can you say that? It's been horrible! Where have you been?"

"I already told you. I'm ready to drop. But we've got to keep working to get out of here."

"It's no use, Daniel. That snow plow was our last hope, and he covered us over." She collapsed against the car, crying.

Daniel put his arm around her. "I can't let you give up, Yo-Yo. The roads are plowed both ways now. We can make it. I can get back to the gas station I saw on Route Twelve. It's several miles, but I know I can make it. With clear roads and taking my time, I'll get there."

Back in the car Jim advised against it. "At least not until you've rested and changed into some fresh, dry clothes. How'd the boots work out?"

"Fine. A little awkward. But you were right: I would have frozen in anything else."

"We're right back where we started from," Yolanda said.

"What do you mean?" Jim asked. His whiskers were starting to show after having missed his morning shave.

"We're all here in this stuck car and there's no way out."

"Sure there is! Like Dan says, the roads are clear. I just don't know if Daniel can make that long trip again. And I'm sorry, but I don't remember how far that gas station is."

Daniel changed his clothes and enjoyed the warmth and comfort of the car. Jim trembled every time the engine was off, but they turned it off more frequently now because there was just an eighth of a tank of gas left.

"Dan," Jim said weakly, his eyes closed.

"Yeah?"

"It may get dark early again tonight. You don't want to be out in the dark."

58

"You mean I've gotta go now?"

"Pretty soon."

"Oh, boy."

"I know, Dan. I'm sorry. But I need help. If I thought Yolanda could make it, I'd send her. But we can't risk it. I'll make it up to you someday."

"Make it up to me? You'd do the same for me, wouldn't you?"

"What do you think?"

"I know. That's why you don't even have to think about making it up to me. I just want you to stay alive and keep from bleeding too much until a doctor can help you. I want to watch you play basketball at State."

"So do I," Jim said, almost asleep. "So, much as I hate to say it, you'd better get going."

11

Phone, Sweet Phone?

Within a hundred feet of the car, Daniel was already so weary he didn't know whether he could go on. He thrust his hands deep into his pockets and slowed down. He took small, steady steps. He decided that he would walk like that the whole way.

And he did. Until he came to the hills. Then he took his hands out of his pockets so he could swing his arms to help him get up the hills. The walking was a lot better and faster than it had been the first time he'd walked this direction. But he still wished the whole thing would be over and that he could sleep in his own bed that night.

He wondered if he would be walking back to Jim's car again. Or this time would he have a ride in a police car or a wrecker or a snow plow? If he made it to the gas station, what would he say? If no one was there, whom would he call? He had lots of time to think about it. Mostly he worried about Jim. If Jim was OK, Yolanda would be OK. If something happened to Jim, then he would have to worry about Yolanda.

By trying not to think about anything, Daniel made the

time pass faster. He decided just to keep walking at that same pace, body upright and steady, hands in his pockets. He kept his eyes trained on objects straight ahead of him. He didn't stop or slow down or look for anything.

But when he came to the top of the last hill before Route Twelve, he had to stop. He had pushed his tiredness from his mind, but the sound of small engines made him wait. He looked over the horizon until he spotted the source of the noise.

It looked like three kids on little three-wheeled motorcyles. They were buzzing all over, sliding around corners, spraying snow high in the air. If only he could get to them, he could get a ride to one of their homes and use their phone!

But they were so far away. They couldn't even see him from where they were. He didn't know whether to try to yell at them or wave at them or head across the field toward them. He tried all three, but their engines were so loud, and they were yelling and laughing so much, they didn't hear him.

And when they finally saw him, rather than stopping or coming over to him, they just waved back. He ran faster, waving more frantically. But they just waved some more and kept curling in bigger and bigger circles.

"God," Daniel prayed, "please let them hear me. Make them stop!"

The kids almost immediately started coming toward Daniel. But he quickly realized they weren't going to stop. They buzzed past him, laughing and coming closer and closer. He yelled, "Stop! Please! I need your help! I need to get to a phone."

But they just laughed more and more. Daniel was frantic. He hadn't been so close to getting help since they'd slid into the ditch. He couldn't let these kids get away. One of the boys about his age came closer to him again. Instead of jumping out of the way, Daniel lunged at him and caught him by the neck with both arms.

The three-wheeler was going so fast that it just threw

Daniel into the snow, and he rolled. The kid on the cycle looked scared and angry. He fishtailed in a big circle and headed straight for Daniel again.

Daniel knew he meant business this time. He had only a split second to decide that he was going to lunge at him again. If they all wanted to beat him up, that was all right. He could at least explain the trouble he was in.

The cycle bore down on him. Daniel leaped toward the driver, who expertly swerved at the last instant. Daniel flopped onto the ground and lay there. He knew he had lost his last chance. The driver of the cycle knew that if he charged Daniel again, Daniel would jump right into his lap. So the kids all scooted away, laughing and waving and pointing.

Slowly, he trudged back to Toboggan Road and kept walking toward Route Twelve. When he finally reached the four-wheel-drive truck in the ditch, no one was around. He needed a break from the wind and cold again, but he didn't want to take too much time.

He crawled in through the hole in the window. He sat there for about five minutes, trying to take the edge off the chill that had taken hold of his body..

As he was crawling out, trying to get to the gas station before dark, he heard the three-wheelers coming. He tried to hide so that he could jump out and surprise them and maybe tell them his story before they took off. But they saw him and quickly turned, heading the other direction.

Daniel kicked at the truck and the ground. Then he climbed out of the ditch and walked down Route Twelve. The only tracks he noticed in the road were the fat, wide tracks of the three-wheelers, the wide impression of a snow-mobile, and the big treads of the snow plow. Still no cars had tried this road.

The shadows grew long. Daniel rounded the bend where earlier in the day he had first heard the snow plow. This time he heard something else. It was the low whirring chop of a helicopter. He squinted into the sky and saw it, a big black machine moving over his head and down the road behind him.

He yelled and waved. But he had no hope of being noticed. The kids on the three-wheelers had gone back to the truck in the ditch and were playing on and in it. As the helicopter whizzed out of sight, Daniel shrugged and kept moving. He thought about praying that God would send that helicopter down Toboggan Road, but it seemed too late.

Half an hour later, as dusk was settling, Daniel arrived at the big gas station. It was closed. No one was in sight. The cars parked in front of its garage doors were buried. Huge drifts had filled in between the pumps. Daniel, heartsick, looked around. And there it was. A pay phone. Inside.

He struggled through the snow and tried the doors. Locked tight. He looked for something he could use to break the glass. Buried in the snow with one end rising out of the drift was an air hose. Daniel pulled and pulled until the rubber cable was completely off the ground. On the end was a metal nozzle.

The hose was hard to straighten out because it was frozen. But Daniel swung it over his head a few times and let it fly through the glass of the front door. Then he reached in and opened the door.

The heat was off, and it was cold inside the office. Daniel dug into his pockets for some change and popped it into the pay phone. The dial tone was a welcome sound. But no matter what he dialed, he still heard the tone. He banged on the phone and clicked the lever several times. Still, he heard that tone.

Finally his coins dropped into the box, and the tone disappeared. He put more money in, dialed the operator and information and the emergency number. Still, the tone. He clicked the receiver ten times before he heard something other than the dial tone.

It was ringing! He waited and waited. When it was

answered, a voice said, "I'm sorry, all circuits are busy now. Please try your call later. This is a recording." Daniel slammed down the phone. He was out of coins. He kicked the nearest thing to him, which was a metal waste basket. It flew toward the door and shattered what was left of the glass. Daniel began to cry. What was the use?

Mad as he was, he still knew he didn't want to walk too far after dark. He headed out to go back down Route Twelve toward Toboggan Road. From behind him came the sound of an engine. He turned in time to see a snowmobile sliding around the curve. *I'll stop him if it kills me*, Daniel decided.

He stood directly in the path of the speeding machine. When the driver swerved left, Daniel jumped right in front of him. The driver swerved back to the right, narrowly missing Daniel.

The man swore.

"What in the world were you doing, kid? I was doing over forty miles an hour!"

"I need help!" Daniel whined. "My brother and sister are stranded in a car on Toboggan Road! My brother's hurt, and our car's in a ditch!"

"You walked all the way from there?" the man asked, pushing his cap back on his head and getting off the snowmobile.

"Twice!"

"Well, you're in luck. I'm Sergeant Bob Sanders with the sheriff's police. And we got a helicopter report of some kids vandalizing a truck in a ditch at the corner up here. Jump on, and I'll go run them off, then we'll see about your brother and sister."

Daniel nearly collasped. He tucked himself in behind the policeman, who was a short, stocky, dark-haired man with a badge on his black leather jacket. "Just put your head on my back," the man said as they raced away. Daniel was glad he said that. He was so tired, it would have been hard to hold his head up as they bounced along.

He carefully lay his head between Sergeant Sanders's

shoulder blades and wrapped his arms around his waist. "My dad's name is Bob, too!" Daniel called out, not knowing whether to laugh or cry.

"That so?" the sergeant said. "Hang on!"

12
Airlift Home

It amazed Daniel how fast he and Sergeant Bob Sanders reached the corner of Route Twelve and Toboggan Road. The kids on the three-wheelers saw them coming, but they didn't have time to get back on their cycles and get away.

"Hold it right there, boys!" Sanders said. "Why, Bobby! My own son! What're you doing here? And Steve! And Phil!"

"Just playing."

"Playing! I got a report that said you were vandalizing this truck. Let's have a look."

"The window's busted out and the radio thing is off the hook. But we didn't do it, Dad. Honest!"

The policeman swore again. "I'll *bet!* I'll deal with you at home, young man. Now get going! And you other two, I'll be talking to your dads!"

"Wait a minute," Daniel said. "These guys didn't do anything to this truck. I did."

"What?"

Daniel told him the whole story. "And I broke the glass at the gas station down the road there, too. I had to get in and use the phone. You understand, don't you?"

" 'Course I do. And thanks for being honest. I'll handle both of these for you. I know the station owner and the owner of this truck, and they've both got insurance. You were just doing what you had to do."

"Thanks."

"You were stranded?" Bobby Sanders asked. Daniel nodded.

"Hey, we're sorry. We thought that was your property and that you were trying to run us off. That's why we didn't stop and were teasing you. You sure could have got us in trouble over this truck if you'd wanted to get even."

"There was no need for that," Daniel said. "But please, Sergeant, can we get to my brother and sister right away?"

"Sure. Let's go."

They flew down Toboggan Road and covered the three and a half miles in just minutes. Daniel pointed to the buried car, and the sergeant slid right up next to it. Already Yolanda was squealing and bouncing in her seat. "Daniel, Daniel! You got help! Oh, Daniel!"

Sergeant Sanders knelt in the front seat with his flashlight and examined Jim's leg. "You're a big one, aren't you?"

Jim didn't respond. He was pale, and his breathing was shallow.

"I'm afraid he's in shock," the policeman said. "We've got to get him out of here. He's not going to fit in any of our vehicles. And this one's not going anywhere."

He grabbed his walkie-talkie and radioed, "Special unit nineteen to airborne three, over."

The staticky response was quick. "This is three. Go ahead."

"My ten-twenty is Toboggan Road, three and half miles from Twelve. Need immediate airborne evacuation of accident victim, over."

"Roger. My E.T.A. is three minutes."

Yolanda got out of the car and hugged Daniel. "You know what Jim kept saying the last half hour, Daniel?"

"What?"

67

"You won't believe it."

" 'Course I will. What?"

"He kept praying. And then he tried to teach me a verse. Isaiah forty: thirty-one. He repeated it over and over until I got it. Then he wanted me to keep saying it. 'Say it for Daniel,' he kept saying. 'Say it for Daniel.' "

"What was it, Yo-Yo?"

"It went like this, 'They that wait upon the Lord shall renew their strength; they shall mount up with wings as eagles; they shall run, and not be weary; and they shall walk, and not faint.' "

"Wow," Daniel said. "That's a promise from God. And now it's coming true. More than that, Yo-Yo. I ran and walked today. I can't say I didn't get weary, but God was with me and protected me. And did you hear who the policeman was talking to on the radio?"

"No."

"A helicopter."

"Really? I didn't hear him say that."

"That's what he meant by 'airborne.' A helicopter is coming!"

The helicopter landed in the road, and Jim was removed from the car on a stretcher. Daniel and Yolanda rode along as he was flown to a nearby hospital. It was from there that Daniel was able to reach his pastor by phone. The pastor listened to the whole story and checked with high school officials to find out exactly where the cheerleading clinic was. "Jim would know," Daniel explained. "But he's sleeping."

To Daniel and Yolanda's surprise, they were both put to bed in the hospital, too. Daniel was treated for what they called "exposure." That simply meant that the skin around his eyes and mouth had been too cold for too long.

They both enjoyed a light, hot meal. Then they got a phone call from their parents. Daniel carefully told them everything that had gone on, from beginning to end. He included the way he had acted when Jim said they weren't going to go.

"You learned a valuable lesson, didn't you, Dan?" his father said.

"Yes, sir."

"We're proud of you," his mother said. "Both of you."

"Don't be proud of me," Yolanda chimed in. "I was a crybaby."

"I'm sure it was difficult. Now you'd better let us talk to the doctor about Jim."

Within three weeks after surgery to repair his leg, Jim was hobbling around on crutches. And he was talking by phone every day with his future college basketball coach. "They told me I had a choice," Jim joked. "They could take the foot off or make the leg as good as new."

"What did you choose?" the coach asked.

"I told them to do both!"

There was some doubt as to whether Jim would be able to go 100 percent when basketball season opened. But the coach assured him there would be no pressure for him to perform well from the beginning. "We'll take our time and be sure you're healthy," he said.

Jim and Daniel and Yolanda were closer than ever after that. They were glad he was going to college in their home state.

"You won't be too far away," Yolanda said.

"I don't ever want to be too far from you, Yo-Yo," he said. "Or from this guy," he added, grabbing Daniel and pulling him close. "The kid was saved my life."

Moody Press, a ministry of the Moody Bible Institute,
is designed for education, evangelization, and edification.
If we may assist you in knowing more about Christ
and the Christian life, please write us without obligation:
Moody Press, c/o MLM, Chicago, Illinois 60610.